First published in hardback in Great Britain by Andersen Press Ltd in 1993
First published in paperback by Picture Lions in 1994
New edition published by Collins Picture Books in 2001
This edition published by HarperCollins Children's Books in 2007

1 3 5 7 9 10 8 6 4 2

ISBN-13: 978-0-00-778250-5

Picture Lions and Collins Picture Books are imprints of HarperCollins Publishers Ltd.
HarperCollins Children's Books is a division of HarperCollins Publishers Ltd.

Text and illustrations copyright © Tony Ross 1993, 2001

Visit our website at: www.harpercollins.co.uk

Printed and bound by South China Printing Co.Ltd

I Want To Be

Tony Ross

HarperCollins *Children's Books*

"The time has come to grow up,"
thought the Little Princess.

"I wonder how I should do it?
Perhaps I should be different."

"But what sort of different should I be?"

"That's not what I should be. I'd better ask Mum."

"What is the best way to be?" she asked.
"Be kind..." said her mother,

"...like your father."

"What is the best way to be?" the Little Princess asked.
"Be loving," said her father,

"...like your mother."

"What is the best way to be?" the Little Princess asked.

"Be clean," said the Cook.

"There is such a lot to remember,"
thought the Little Princess.
"I must be kind, loving and clean."

"What is the best way to be?" the Little Princess asked.

"Be brave," said the General.

"Be brave," thought the Little Princess.
"That's it! Then I could get the spiders
out of the bath myself."

"What is the best way to be?" the Little Princess asked.

"Be good at swimming..." said the Admiral,

"...then you will be safe if your boat ever sinks."

"What is the best way to be?" the Little Princess asked.

"Be clever," said the Prime Minister.

"And be healthy," said the Doctor.

"Oh dear!" thought the Little Princess.
"I must be kind, loving and clean, brave, good at swimming,
clever and healthy. I haven't got that many fingers!"

"Growing up is SO difficult."

"What is the best way to be?" asked the Little Princess.

"Oh, I don't know," said the Maid.

"I suppose the important question is...
what do YOU want to be?"

"I want to be..."

"TALL," said the Little Princess.

"But you ARE tall," said the Little Prince.

Collect all the funny stories featuring the demanding Little Princess!

I Want My Potty — Tony Ross — 978-0-00-723621-8

I Want To Be — Tony Ross — 978-0-00-724282-5

I Want My Dinner — Tony Ross — 978-0-00-723620-6

I Want A Sister — Tony Ross — 978-0-00-724281-8

I Don't Want To Go To Hospital — Tony Ross — 978-0-00-710957-9

I Want My Dummy — Tony Ross — 978-0-00-724283-2

I Don't Want To Wash My Hands — Tony Ross — 978-0-00-715072-4

I Want My Tooth — Tony Ross — 978-0-00-724365-5

I Don't Want To Go To Bed — Tony Ross — 978-0-00-719478-0

I Want My Mum — Tony Ross — 978-0-00-720033-1

I Want A Friend — Tony Ross — 978-0-00-721491-4

"The Little Princess has huge appeal to toddlers and Tony Ross's illustrations are brilliantly witty."
Practical Parenting

Tony Ross was born in London in 1938. His dream was to work with horses but instead he went to art college in Liverpool. Since then, Tony has worked as an art director at an advertising agency, a graphic designer, a cartoonist, a teacher and a film maker – as well as illustrating over 250 books!